Wheels, Wheels, Wheels

by Nancy White Carlstrom
Illustrated by Roni Shepherd

ScottForesman
A Division of HarperCollinsPublishe

D1307493

Big cars, brown cars

rolling through the town cars

Big trucks, white trucks

rolling through the night trucks

Big trains, black trains

rolling on the track trains

Car wheels, truck wheels

wheels on trains

Rolling in the sunshine

Rolling in the rain

Round and round

fast and slow

Wheels are rolling

there they go

Rolling along

singing a song

Zoom brr-room

Zoom brr-room

Wheels, wheels, wheels.